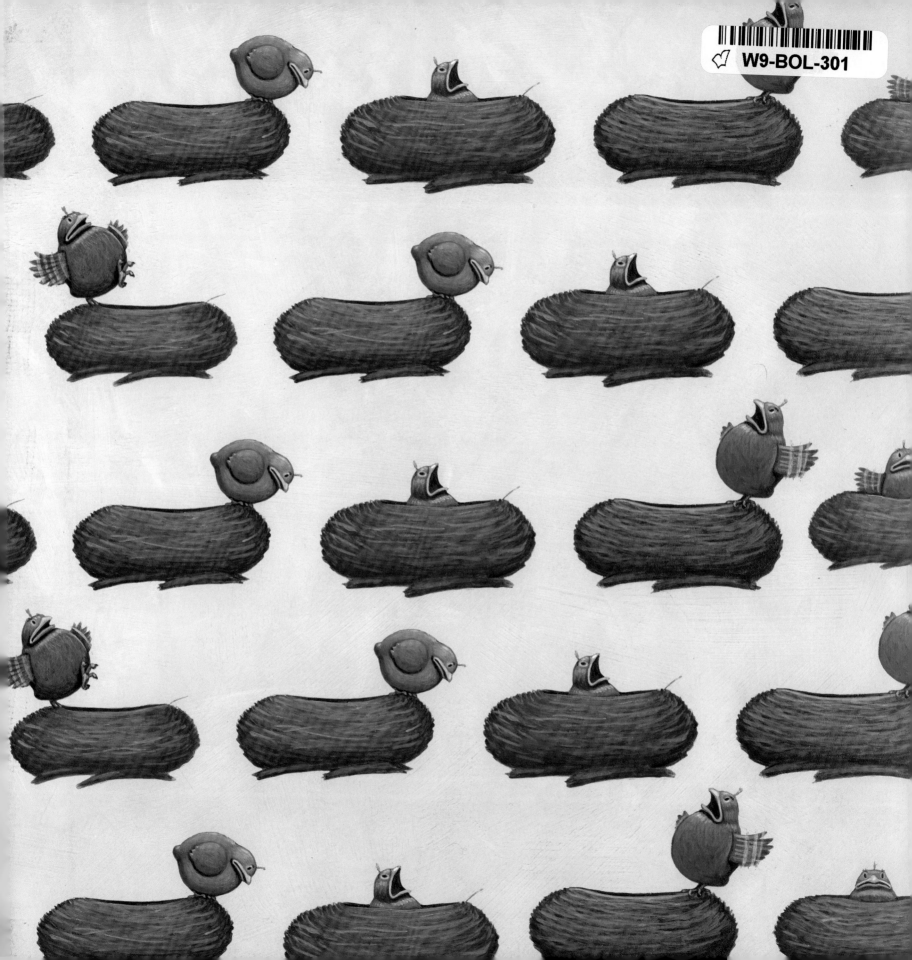

to Kester and Ava

BEACH LANE BOOKS
An imprint of Simon & Schuster Children's Publishing Division
1230 Avenue of the Americas, New York, New York 10020
Copyright © 2019 by Mark Teague
All rights reserved, including the right of reproduction
in whole or in part in any form.
BEACH LANE BOOKS is a trademark of Simon & Schuster, Inc.
For information about special discounts for bulk purchases, please contact Simon &
Schuster Special Sales at 1-866-506-1949 or business@simonandschuster.com.
The Simon & Schuster Speakers Bureau can bring authors to your live event. For more
information or to book an event, contact the Simon & Schuster Speakers Bureau at
1-866-248-3049 or visit our website at www.simonspeakers.com.
Book design by Sonia Chaghatzbanian
The illustrations for this book were rendered in acrylics.
Manufactured in China
0719 SCP
First Edition
2 4 6 8 10 9 7 5 3 1
Library of Congress Cataloging-in-Publication Data
Names: Teague, Mark, author, illustrator.
Title: Fly! / Mark Teague.
Description: First edition. | New York : Beach Lane Books, [2019] | Summary: Mama bird
wants Baby bird to learn to fly so he can migrate with the rest of the flock, but Baby bird
would rather go by hot air balloon or car, instead.
Identifiers: LCCN 2019008861 | ISBN 9781534451285 (hardback) | ISBN 9781534451292
(ebook)
Subjects: | CYAC: Birds—Fiction. | Animals—Infancy—Fiction. | Flight—Fiction. |
Humorous stories. | BISAC: JUVENILE FICTION / Animals / Birds. | JUVENILE
FICTION / Social Issues / New Experience. | JUVENILE FICTION / Humorous Stories.
Classification: LCC PZ7.T2193825 Fly 2019 | DDC [E]—dc23 LC record available at
https://lccn.loc.gov/2019008861

fly!

Mark Teague

BEACH LANE BOOKS

New York   London   Toronto   Sydney   New Delhi

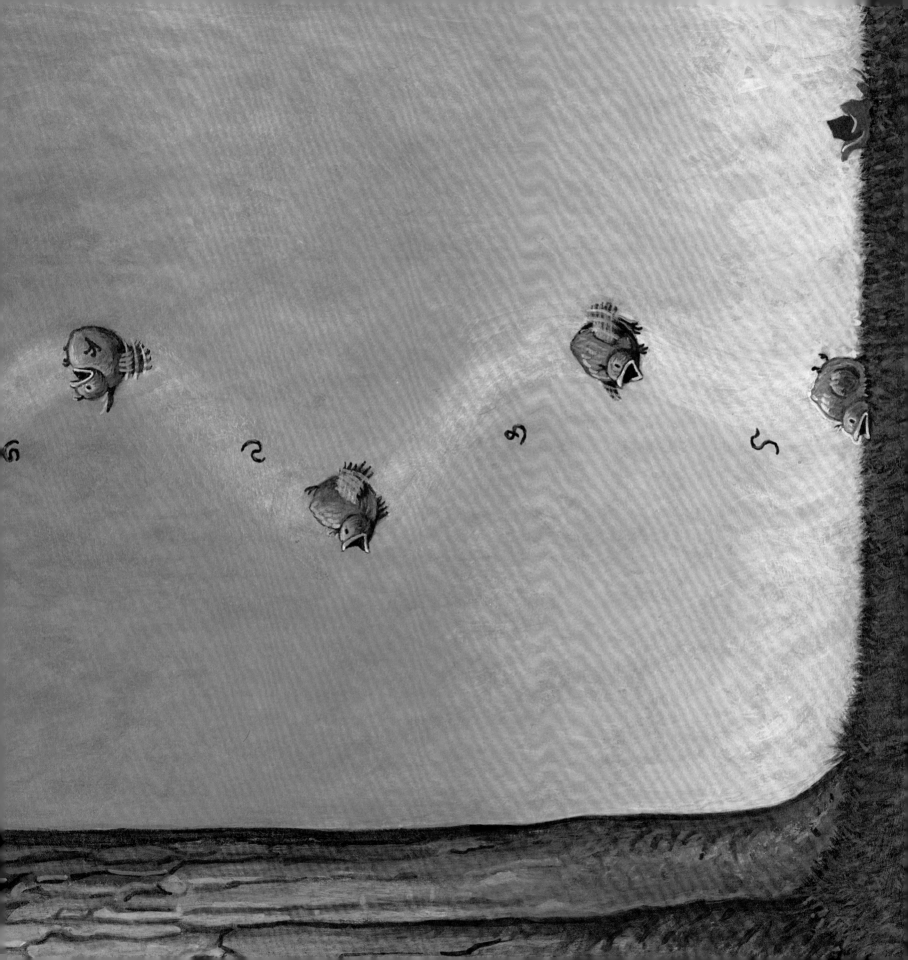